Prison 456

Samantha Nicklaus

This is a work of fiction. Any resemblance to actual persons, living or dead, or actual events is purely coincidental.

Reviews can be left on Amazon.com and GoodReads.com

SamanthaNicklaus.com

Twitter.com/SamNicklaus

Facebook.com/AuthorSamNicklaus

Copyright © 2017 by Samantha Nicklaus

Logo by Ren Oliveira

All rights reserved. This book or any portion thereof may not be reproduced or used in any manner whatsoever without the express written permission of the author except for the use of brief quotations in a book review.

This book is dedicated to my incredible siblings, Kelsey and Billy Reavy, Biggie Smalls, and Andy McLegs, our beloved dog Rusty, and anyone and everyone who enjoyed Prison 917.

Part One 1

Part Two 39

Part Three 69

Part One

A sharp light woke me up. Even before I opened my eyes, I could tell that the light was *too* bright. Slowly, squinting, I peeked my eyes open, then quickly closed again.

Electricity.

For half a second, I thought that Prison 917 was a dream. I had eaten too much cheese before bed or took some kind of sleeping pill. Now I was going to wake up and tell my mom all about it, and she would tell me to take better care of myself.

I prepared myself this time and peeked my eyes open again.

No.

It was a white cinderblock wall in front of me. I let my eyes adjust and rolled over. I had no idea why I kept doing this. Expecting the best, I mean. *When had the best ever happened to me?* I took in a breath. *Alright, that was a bit dramatic. I had the best for* most *of my life.*

I went to sit up and realized I was sore. Not sore like after a workout sore, but sore like I had been hit by a bus. I moved each finger, each toe, each limb, one by one to see what hurt. Pretty much everything. The cot I was on was somehow felt harder than the dirt in Delany's house I was used to.

Delany.

I sat upright, or as upright as I could. On the other side of the bed was the same white cinderblock walls, with a tiny sink and a tiny toilet, maybe four feet away from me. *This* was a prison. This was what I thought of when I thought of prison. I looked at the other wall, and sure enough, thick metal bars stood there, caging me in.

I got to my feet and went to the bars. I had gotten up too quickly, and my vision went black for a second. I held onto the bars. As my vision came back, I realized there was nothing on the other side of the bars, just another white cinderblock wall. "Hello?" I called. The place was silent. "Hello? Delany?"

I heard someone grumble in the cell next to me. "Hey! Hey, are you from the prison too? 917? Hello?"

They didn't say anything, and no one else called back. I went and sat down on the cot, trying to figure out how I got here.

I blacked out, I thought. *Why? I got hit on the head. I fell and hit my head. I was drugged. I was beaten.*

Those all seemed equally as likely. Delany had been right next to me. What if one of the infected got her? What if they killed her and it was all my fault?

I got up and went to the bars again. I put my face up against the cold metal, trying to will myself to see further down the hallway.

After a few minutes, I sat back down. It was silent here, eerily silent. The other prison had never been quiet. I wasn't used to it. I started to think that maybe I was all alone here, that someone had forgotten me, and I would slowly starve to death, all alone.

I stood up again and tried to take in a few deep breaths. My heart was racing. "Okay, okay," I said to myself, "it's okay. It's okay. We're okay." I shook my hands out like the band kids used to do before they would play to "limber up". I thought it was funny then, but for some reason, that's all I could do now. I shook my dead-weighted hands until my wrists hurt. "Okay, okay, I'm okay. Delany is okay. We're all okay. It's okay."

A guard walked by and I nearly jumped out of my skin. "Hey!" I called, running up to the bars. He was a few feet away, but he stopped when he heard me, like a deer in headlights. I wrapped my hands around the bars. "Please, please come here."

He looked above my cell, then gingerly took a few steps towards me. "Hey, I'm Heather," I said, as calmly as I could. I could still feel my heart beating through my chest. I'm sure my entire body was shaking with the force of it. "I'm not dangerous, I just want to know how we got here and if my friends are okay."

"They got you from the other prison," the guard said, in a whisper. "Everyone who survived is here." He went to take a step away, and I tried to grab for him. I wouldn't have reached him either way, but he took a step back.

"Sorry," I said taking in a breath, "sorry. My friend, Delany. Is she here?" He looked at me, blinked, then walked down the hallway with me screaming after him.

"Heather?"

I stopped screaming. It was Pittman. My heart soared. "Pitt?" I called back. It sounded like he was in the cell to my right. "Are you okay?" I scooted down to the right side of my cell, putting my arms as far out of the bars as I could.

"Groggy as all hell," he said. I could hear the cot creak as he stood up. "What the fuck is going on?"

"They moved us to a real prison," I said. "The guard told me everyone who survived the infected is here."

"How many is that?"

I paused. "I only saw four people get attacked."

It was silent for a few seconds, and then Pitt grunted. "If I had known we only had to let four goddamn people die to get fucking running water, I would have let those yellow fuckers out myself," he said. "Good work, Red. Do you know where George is?"

"No, I haven't spoken to anyone but you. Do you know if Delany is okay?" I asked him. Of course, I knew there was no way he could, but I had to ask. Pitt grunted again. "I guess I'll wait until someone else wakes up." I could hear his water start running. Or maybe he was just peeing.

I sat back down on the cot. Did they come to save us because of the infected? It would have made sense. I mean, eventually, the infected would have killed all of us anyway. Probably. Delany had told me that they weren't sure anymore how the infection even spread after a person caught it, they just did what the people before them did.

But *walls. A roof. Water.* This was a huge change. And Pittman was right, this was for the better. Maybe. Part of me felt better here. It was safe, there were guards. I didn't have to worry about anyone attacking me, or starving to death. There were going to be rules here. Though I had seen some after-school specials about abuse in prison. But we were just kids, right? And how much worse could it get?

I took in a deep breath. It was too much at once. I decided to be grateful for what I had at the moment, and worry about the rest later. First order of business was to find Delany. After that, she would work something out.

I laid back down on the cot and replayed what happened in my mind. The burnings, Rue dying, us running. It felt like a dream, like something I watched happen to someone else, not me. It wasn't supposed to happen that way. They were supposed to cave, to help us rebuild after the storm. I didn't expect Rue to play chicken with us for so long. I didn't expect the infected to get out. I didn't expect anyone to die because of this. Because of *me*.

Other people started waking up, and I could hear them yelling. Some of them yelled for other people, some just screamed wordlessly. Others cursed themselves, God, the guards, anyone they could think of. I'm pretty sure I heard someone curse me. I tried to yell over them, to ask if anyone knew where Delany was, but no one ever answered. Or maybe they did, and I just couldn't hear them over everyone else. Everyone was busy having their own breakdowns.

Eventually, when the screaming reached its peak, there was the static pop of a loudspeaker. "Welcome to your new home." It was a man's voice, but it reminded me of Delany on my first day at 917. "For the first twenty-four hours you are here, we are going to keep you inside of your cells."

Someone yelled back at the voice, a long string of curses. The voice didn't seem to hear him. "We would like you to think of this as your home, and we understand that some of you have never had modern luxuries. Please take these twenty-four hours to adjust. After that, we will let you mingle in a common area as well as give you access to the kitchen."

I thought of Delany. Did she know how to flush a toilet, turn on a sink? I'm not even sure she had ever seen a light bulb.

"While this is your home, we will keep you civil. Anyone who does not follow our rules will be punished, swiftly and severely."

There was a click, and the voice was gone. Some people went back to yelling, but I think most of us calmed down. The lack of food was not going to be an issue. Most of us had gone longer without. Had I been at the prison for four months? Three and a half? It was hard to keep track of the time. Either way, I had lost enough weight that I could count my ribs, see my collarbone. Twenty-four hours without food wouldn't kill any of us.

I must have drifted off to sleep at some point because I woke up to the sound of footsteps. They clicked softly against the cinderblock floors, step after step. Then they stopped. I rolled my head so I could see. A guard standing in front of my cell. "Get up," he said, and I got up. "Stand against the wall."

I backed up until my back touched the wall. He took a ring of keys out of his pocket and unlocked my door. It slid open, and he waited for me to walk through it.

I didn't ask him what was going on, I just followed where he walked. I peeked in the cells and saw a few people I knew. Sandra, George, Rabbit. I was happy to see they were okay, but still, my heart ached with the thought of Delany.

We went down the hall and to a door, where he took a badge that was hanging around his neck and swiped it. The door beeped, and I could hear it unlock. He opened it, and let me outside.

I didn't realize it was daytime. The sun was blinding. I put my hand up, letting my eyes adjust. It was a small fenced in area. I guess small was a relative term, after the prison I had come from. This wasn't that big, but we all could have fit out there. Well, all of us that survived, I guess.

There were about twenty other kids in there, with two guards watching over us in wooden towers on the other side of the fences, guns in hand. It reminded me of the penguin exhibit at the zoo, all the little birds cuddled together. That's how they looked, so close all of them were touching.

"Hey," I said to no one in particular. It looked like the group I had come into the prison with, plus and minus a few people. "What's going on?"

"No idea," said one kid, I think his name was Scott. "They just brought us all out here."

"This is bad." It was Sunja, a dark-skinned girl with hands that were always twisted together in knots.

"No, it's not," I said, trying to comfort them. I walked away from the door and closer to them. "Listen, they probably brought us outside first because we were in the prison the least amount of time. We're the least 'wild' or whatever."

"They said they would let us all out into the common area," someone else said, I couldn't see who. "What if this is all of us?"

"We passed other people on the way out of there."

"What if they are going to kill all of them?"

"What if they are going to kill all of *us*?"

"Why would they rescue us just to—"

"Did you see the guns?

"Someone mentioned a kitchen"

"Whose voice was that before, I—"

Everyone was talking at once, and I lost track of what was being said. I looked around. The fences were tall, with barbed wire on the top, but not electric. The two guards had sniper rifles, nothing that could kill us all at once. The fence wasn't dug into the ground at all, either.

You're thinking about escaping, I thought, shocking myself a little. *Stop it.*

I don't know how long we were outside, probably an hour. The guards watched us but didn't say anything. Eventually, everyone calmed down and talked about the infected, and what they remembered about getting here. No one had seen Delany.

The door opened, and a guard appeared. "Are you going to come inside nicely?" he asked. This was a different guard, one I hadn't seen before. He had a long, black beard.

"Of course," I answered. I was still close to the door, so I turned to everyone else. "We will be nice." It came across as an order, though that's not what I had intended.

"Come on then," the guard said, and we walked inside. We followed a different guard down the hallway, with Black Beard behind us.

People were stopping at cells as we passed. As long as they moved by the time Black Beard got to them, they didn't seem to mind. I stopped at Rabbit's.

He was laying on his cot, shaking. "Coming down?" I asked. He looked at me and smiled.

"*You*. You got us into this shithole," he said, his arm wrapped around his torso, hugging himself. "Thanks a lot." I couldn't tell if he was being sarcastic or not. He sat up a little bit to look at me. "Have you seen Delany? Noel? Obviously not Rue."

I shook my head. "Just Pittman and you." Rabbit gave a quick nod. "Hey, you'll be alright," I said, checking where Black Beard was. I didn't have a lot of time. "If you see Delany—"

"I know. Go," Rabbit said, waving one hand at me. It destabilized him enough that he almost fell back into his cot. I looked at Black Beard, who was only about five feet from me and started to walk again.

George was a few cells down, standing against the bars. "Hey, Pittman is okay," I told him. He reached through the bar and took my hand.

"Thank God," he said, closing his eyes for a second.

"I'll tell him you're okay," I told him, taking my hand back. "I got to go."

"Stay safe, Heather," George said to me. It almost sounded like a prayer.

They brought us into the kitchen. It had tables like an elementary school cafeteria. And food. We could smell food. Also like a school cafeteria, it had a little door that took you to a line in the kitchen, then back out another door to the tables. We lined up, pushing and shoving at each other for a minute before we settled into our places. The guards didn't seem to mind.

Socks was in front of me. I hadn't noticed him outside before. He hadn't come in with my group to the other prison, I didn't know why he was with us. Maybe he had a good record or something. "You doing okay?" he asked me as we waited. Everyone was back to pushing and shoving, trying to see what we were going to eat.

I nodded. "Just worried about some people."

"Delany?"

"Yeah," I said, trying to be casual. "And Noel, Pittman, Freddie, R—" I almost said Rue's name.

"I'm sure they're fine. And hey, not for nothing, but you were part of what got us here," Socks said, tapping my arm. "I don't care what those fucking savages say to you. You three got us a roof, food, and clean water. You did good by us."

"Thanks, Socks," I said. I wanted to say that no, I didn't. I knew we had all of those things now, and some level of safety, even if it was just from each other, but something felt wrong. *A cage is a cage is a cage*, I said to myself.

Burgers.

The smell hit me, and I couldn't help but tear up. Socks stepped into the kitchen, and I peeked around him. I was right. Burgers. They looked gray, with off-yellow buns, but they were burgers. "They shouldn't feed us meat," someone said, a few people up. "Vegetarians get sick all the time when they go back to eating meat."

"Fine, I'll eat yours then," Socks said, and a few people laughed.

We took turns picking up trays, and I silently hoped no one would hit someone else with their tray. We walked down the little line, sliding out trays, while three tired looking old ladies plopped food down on them. Gray burgers with wet looking tatter tots and warm milk.

When I got my food, I sat next to Socks and a few other people, but I didn't listen to them as they talked. I ate my tater-tots, still cold in the middle, and drank my milk. I watched the guards, mostly. There were three in the room, two by the doors and one that wandered around, watching us. I watched his path for a few minutes.

When he wasn't looking, I tore pieces of burger off and shoved it into my pockets. Pittman and Rabbit were close enough to me that I could feed them, too. They had only moved us so far. Who knows when they would move anyone else?

There wasn't a clock in the room or any way to gauge time, aside from the sun outside. I think we had been in the cafeteria maybe an hour. One of the guards, the one who had been wandering around, barked at us to clean up, pointing to a set of garbage cans in the back of the room. No one moved, just stared at him.

He said it again, pointing more forcefully this time, as if we just hadn't understood him.

"Fuck," Socks whispered next to me. I looked around the room. Still, no one was moving.

"Come on," I said to Socks and stood up. I picked up my tray and walked it over to the garbage can. While I was clearing it, Socks came up next to me and did the same.

"They don't look happy," he whispered to me.

"They'll follow our lead, it's alright," I said much more confidently than I felt. We turned around. Everyone was looking at us. I could feel my face getting red.

"Come on," I said, loudly. "Clean your shit up."

Silence.

"Get up," I repeated, louder this time. Two people got up and started walking towards us, then three, then everyone was getting up and walking towards the garbage cans. Socks and I stepped out of the way, and I took in a deep breath.

"Look at you, Red," Socks said with a chuckle. "Stepping up to the plate."

They moved us to another room after that. We didn't pass any more cells, just an empty hallway. We sat down in a room full of chairs, but it was empty aside from that. Guards watched us as we squabbled over who got to sit next to who. Once we sat down, we chatted and joked—it reminded me a lot of high school. The door opened, and a man walked in.

He was distinguished, which is what my mom told me to say instead of old. A long face, with brown and gray hair, a pig looking nose, and a liver spot on his cheek: old. He was wearing a suit, and shoes that clicked like heels as he walked. He stood in front of us, and we fell silent.

"I want to be honest with you," he said. It was the man from the intercom. He linked his hands together in front of him. "I was not in charge of the prison you were at before, Prison 917. That was experimental, run by some of the most evil men I can think of." He paused, looking for our reactions. I don't think we showed much. Evil men didn't surprise us.

"The man who ran your prison, he was fired and jailed for his crimes. We were tasked with taking you in." He looked around the room again.

"Did that involve beating us?" Socks asked, leaning back in his chair. The man cocked his head, but didn't say anything. "Because I have some monster bruises on me."

"We were not responsible for your transport, either," the man said. "And for that, I apologize. We will be giving everyone medical examinations shortly."

"Everyone?" I asked, "or just us right here?"

The man looked at me for a second and looked like he was about to smile. "Everyone. We are taking a larger group outside now, and another to the kitchen."

"My friend Rabbit—Jack," I added. "He needs to be taken to doctor now." The man nodded at me and looked at one of the guards. The guard put his radio to his mouth and mumbled something.

"Anything else?" the man asked me.

"I want all of us together," I said. When he walked in the room, I had thought that he was trying to play us. I wasn't sure how, but he seemed sleazy. I was starting to back down on that. Maybe he cared. *Maybe*.

He nodded, again. "After everyone is fed, and your friend Rabbit is seen to. I promise." He looked away from me and went back to addressing the group. "I have no say in how you got here, whether you are innocent or guilty. I take my job very seriously here, and that job is to care for you. I expect you all to be civil with each other, but I understand that you may have to take some time to get used to that. I understand you were at Prison 917 the least amount of time. Please, remember what manners are like. We have law and order here."

I noticed he didn't say 917 the same way we did. Everyone called it 9-1-7. He called it nine hundred seventeen. I almost wanted to correct him.

He looked at the group for a second, then turned on his heel and strutted away.

"He's fucking weird," Socks said once the door closed and there was a general murmur of agreement.

They took us back to our cells afterward, single file line. As we walked down the row of cells, some of them were empty. Most of them, actually. Seems like Old Guy was going to be true to his word. Rabbit's cell was empty, too. I felt a little better.

We were locked back up, one by one. No one argued much, which I was thankful for. I didn't know what "swiftly and severely" meant in this context, and I knew we were going to find out at some point, but the longer we could put that off, the happier I was.

We sat in our cells for a while, I wasn't sure how long. It was worse than the other prison. We yelled around to each other, trying to talk, but without being able to see each other, it felt awkward and weird.

"I saw George," I told Pittman right away.

"Yeah?" I don't think I have ever heard Pittman excited before. I liked it.

"Yeah, he's okay. He has a bit of a bruise on his cheek, but he's okay," I said. "He was worried about you."

Pittman sighed with relief. He was whispering to himself, and I couldn't really hear him over the noise, but I thought he said, "Oh, my sweet Jewish prince. Thank god."

"Do you want some burger?" I asked him.

"They're going to take me out soon," Pittman said, very sure of himself. He went back to whatever he had been doing before, which I could only assume was pushups or something. I could hear the girl to the left of me peeing. Someone a few cells down wouldn't stop singing to themselves.

"I don't remember everyone being this fucking annoying," Pitt said to me. "This is why fighting works. It stops stupid people from irritating the rest of us. Fuck."

"They said they would let us all out soon," I reminded him. "Just a little bit longer."

"So more people can annoy me?" Pitt said, "Fucking great."

"Well, you're not having a good day," someone—I wasn't sure who, or where they were speaking from—called out.

"Shut the fuck up," Pitt snapped.

Pittman got taken away with another group. I paced around my cell, ran some water over my face, peed. I counted tiles, traced circles on the walls, listened to other people talk. It was boring as all hell waiting like that. I could see why people went crazy in prison.

It might have been an hour later, but all the cell doors opened all at once, and everyone came running out. We were running into each other, trying to figure out where we were, and where everyone else was. It looked like our little group was towards the end of the hallway, so we took off towards the right.

People were running up and down the hallways, screaming names. I saw two people crash into each other and land on their asses, and two other people hug each other so fiercely they fell over. I ran down the hallway, screaming Delany's name.

Of course, she was the only person to have not left her cell. I found her, curled up on her cot, looking like a wounded animal. "Delany?" I said from her cell door. "Hey, it's me."

Her mouth was tucked against her arm. She raised her head, looked up at me, then shoved her head back down. I walked in and sat next to her. "What's going on? Are you okay?"

I put a hand on her back, and she flinched. "This is what you lived with?" she asked me, moving only her eyes to look at me.

I looked around her cell. She had tried to climb everything—I could tell by the streaks of blood around the room. Like a caged animal, she had clawed at the walls. "More or less," I said.

It was occurring to me that whatever I thought was going to happen—an escape, a riot, a happily-ever-after—it was not going to happen with Delany. I rubbed my hand up and down her back.

"Listen, this isn't that bad," I told her. I took half a burger out of my pocket. It was cold now. "Did you eat?"

"What the fuck is that?" she asked me. She sounded like herself for a second.

"Meat," I answered. "From a cow. A burger." I realized she didn't know what a cow was either. "It's good. I ate some."

She looked at me. "I'll have the bread." She uncurled her arms from around herself and took it.

"It's not going to taste like the bread at the prison," I warned her. She ate it anyway. "Do you know how the sink works?" She looked at me. I got up and pulled the handle back. "It's water."

"Water?" she asked, standing up. That gave me more hope. Maybe she could adjust. Everyone else was. True, she was the only one born in the prison, but she had survived this long for a reason.

She stood next to me. "Where does it come from?" She looked at me and blinked.

"We have metal pipes in the ground that carry it from all over," I said, then I pushed the handle off. "You can have as much as you want." She looked at me like I was joking. "I'm serious."

I went through and explained how the toilet worked, how sheets worked, how lights worked. I had to explain everything to her. She took everything in stride, asking me questions. I answered everything I could, about what the toilet was made from, and who "invented" electricity.

"Alright," she said, looking around her cell. "Alright."

"You want to go see everyone else?" I asked her.

"No." It was a flat answer, and one I had expected. I couldn't imagine being exposed to so many new things at once. I thought it might be like being abducted by aliens. I couldn't blame her for being terrified. I took her pillowcase, which she had taken off of the pillow and thrown on the floor, and ran it under the sink. I used it to clean her blood off of the walls.

"Alright," I said, and sat down on her cot. She sat down next to me. "I was really worried about you, you know."

"I heard," Delany said. "They took Rabbit past me."

"Is he okay?"

"Who cares?"

I stopped and looked at her. "The doctor came out and told me he would be fine," she said. We sat in silence for a few breaths. "So, how are we getting out of here?"

I looked at her. "Out?"

Delany looked at me like I had grown another head. "Yeah, *out*. How are we getting home?"

Home. She wanted to go back? "Delany, I think this is for good," I said, shaking my head. "We've got food and water, and a roof over our heads. I don't think that's an option."

"Of course it is," Delany said, standing up. "Half the kids in our prison where there because they broke out of prisons like this, and you're three times as smart as them. Do you not want to go home?" It was accusatory, like I was betraying her.

"A cage is a cage is a cage," I said with a sigh.

"What?" Delany asked.

"It's an expression, I guess," I said. "It doesn't matter. Listen, we aren't innocent, we—"

"*I'm* not innocent?" Delany said, her voice cracking, she got so loud so suddenly. "Me?" We looked at each other for a few seconds.

"I didn't mean you," I corrected. "I know you didn't do anything to end up there."

"What did you do?" she asked. "What did Pitt? Rabbit? Byrdie?" Byrdie's name stung like a brand on my cheek. "Did they deserve *that*?"

I wanted to point out that Pittman did kill someone, and even though it was allegedly to stop a dog fighting ring, he still did kill someone. So did Byrdie, even if she was only six. Rabbit's drugs caused four overdoses. And he escaped from another prison.

"Look," I said, calmly, standing up to meet her. "Just— let's settle in first. Get a feel for the place. Then we'll think about getting out." I wanted to mention that she wouldn't even leave her cell yet, how did she think she was going to get out of the entire prison, but I kept that to myself.

Whatever Delany thought of that idea, she didn't let me know. A stiff "get out" was all I got. I left her cell and went down the hall to the common room, where everyone else had been ushered.

Now that Delany was okay, I checked up on a few other people. Rabbit was with a doctor, but I found Pittman and George, and Freddie, and a few other people. Pittman put a hand on the top of my head the second I saw him. "You," he said, smiling. "It's been years since I've seen running water." Pittman, for the first time in a long time, didn't have his pink X painted across his chest. I almost didn't recognize him with a shirt on.

George smiled at me. "You're a good kid, you know that, Heather?"

I wasn't sure how things were going to go. Delany, Noel, and I were responsible for this. No matter what that Old Man had said, as far as anyone was concerned, the three of us got us here. I didn't know how that was going to go over. So far, so good.

Freddie shook her head a little. "I knew you would be the downfall of my business," she said, flashing a smirk.

"Have you guys seen Noel?" I asked. Pitt took his hand off of my head. He licked his lips slowly. He looked at George.

"We thought you knew," George said slowly. He held out his hand and Pittman took it.

"What happened?" I asked, looking at him. He looked down at the ground. My heart started to race. "Pitt?"

"She, ugh, didn't make it," he said.

"What?" I squeaked.

"An infected got her," Freddie said. Even she looked a little upset. "Right before they came to get us."

I shook my head. "No, no. She was right next to me, we were in the front, we—" I stopped. The last thing I remember was running. Delany had my hand, Noel was in front of me, Delany yanking me towards her, off to the side—she had pulled me out of the way. The infected must have grabbed Noel instead of me.

"Fuck," I whispered. "Fuck."

Pittman nodded a little. "This is what she would have wanted. You and Delany got us here. After all those years of living in the dirt, you did this." George reached out to put his hand on my shoulder, shaking me a little. "Noel would have wanted this for us."

The loudspeaker crackled. "Please return to your cells for the night." It was the Old Man's voice again. Another crack, and silence. No one moved, we kept talking, lounging about. George tapped my arm.

"Do you think we should go?" he asked me. Pitt had slunk a few feet away, talking to another Pink I didn't know the name of.

I looked around the room. The guards were looking at each other as well, wondering what was going to happen. I could get a group of kids to throw out some garbage. Get three hundred plus to get into cages in an orderly fashion? Not a chance.

Freddie was standing next to me, her back against the wall. "Hey," I said, "Do you think Blue's still with you?"

She scoffed. "Of course."

"Think you can get them to willingly walk back into their cells?"

She hesitated. "Most of them, yeah."

"Good."

I didn't have to say anything, George had already gotten Pitt's attention. I could maybe get Red, but with Rabbit gone and Noel dead, Yellow and Orange were out. Brock was— I realized I hadn't seen Brock. I turned back to Freddie.

"Brock?"

Freddie looked around the room. "Last I saw him, he was fighting one of the guys who picked us up. I guess he didn't make it."

Alright, so out of seven, we have three. Two and a half, really.

Across the room, I could see Cassidy, flipping her hair and laughing. "Go start telling Blue to go to bed," I said over my shoulder to Freddie as I walked away from her. I made a beeline for Cassidy.

"Hey," she chirped as I walked up. "How are you doing?" Her smile was unsettling, but the other Green's around her didn't seem to mind.

"Hey, do you know what happened to Brock?" I asked.

The Green next to Cassidy, I had no idea what their name was, shook their head. "He didn't get out."

"I'm sorry," I said, and I meant it. Brock wasn't much of a thinker, but he didn't seem like a bad guy. "And Cassidy, you're his second?" Cassidy made a face at me, I had no idea what it was supposed to convey. "Listen, I'm sure you guys don't want to start a fight with these guards. If we don't get back into the cells soon, they're going to force us."

"You want us to tell Green to listen to some guards?" Cassidy asked me. It was the first time I had heard her voice something other than undying enthusiasm.

I wasn't even going to pretend. "You have to," I said. They looked at each other for a second. "Blue, Red, and Pink are leaving. Orange is going to follow Red, and Yellow probably will too. Do you really want to fight a bunch of guards with Purple?"

"But if Yellow didn't go—"

"They have guns."

"Green isn't about cells."

"I don't—"

"I mean I think we—"

"Yeah."

Cassidy looked at me. "I'll spread the word, but no promises."

I gave her my most charming smile. "That's all I can ask for."

That left Purple, who wasn't going to go it alone. I could live with that. I looked around. It had been maybe five minutes since the loudspeaker cracked out orders. The guards were stopping anyone who got close to them and telling them to get back to their cells. They weren't being aggressive, yet.

Two Reds walked past me. "You guys gotta go to bed," I told them. "We're not fighting the guards."

They looked at me like I was a toddler who had told them to buy me a pony. "Yeah, okay," the girl said.

"I'm not kidding," I snapped. "Get your ass in your cell."

"Or?" the boy quipped.

"Or I'll kick your ass. Go." It was the first time I had ever truly threatened anyone. The boy scoffed at me, but as they walked away, they changed direction and went towards the door.

"Slow but steady."

I turned around to Socks. He smiled at me. "Look at you," he said. "Our little girl, all grown up. To think, just a few short months ago you were all doe-eyed, carrying a dead body to a mass grave."

I ignored him. "Can you help me get the Reds back?" I asked.

"Back on your side, or back into cages?" He asked.

"How about both?" I tried.

"I'll try for the cages, but you're on your own with the rest of it," he said.

"Thank you," I said as he walked away.

Freddie was already getting Blue's out the door. Pitt had gotten all of the Pinks, at least from what I could tell. He and George were talking to a few Green's. Slowly, only a handful of people at a time, were wandering towards the door. No one wanted to admit that they were doing what they were told, but we had a point; there was no winning a fight against armed guards.

Eventually, we were down to about thirty people. From what I could tell, they were mostly Yellows with a few Purple's sprinkled in. Pittman looked at me. "Do I start busting heads, or?" he asked.

I looked around. The guards were moving closer and closer to us, forming a circle. They were going slowly, being very casual about it. I looked at the Yellows. From how they were—both in general and in that moment— they looked ready for a fight.

"Fuck," I said.

"Yeah, I think I'm out," Freddie said. "Good luck with all of this." She slinked off, more than happy to be rid of us.

Pittman leaned over and kissed George.

"You go too," he said. George hesitated for a second, then followed after Freddie.

Socks, Pittman, and I stood there, watching the guards close in. "Do we really want to be a part of this?" Socks asked.

"No, but I want to make sure the guards don't hurt them," I said. There were seven guards. Seven guards and thirty of them. Tasers, pepper spray, guns, and handcuffs. Fists. It was an uneven fight. Still, with their numbers, I was almost worried for the guards.

We were by the door, and the guards didn't bother us. They were focused on the Yellows, who started to get closer and closer to each other as the guards moved in.

"Excuse me."

I hadn't heard his shoes clicking this time. The Old Man was behind us, in the doorway. We moved, and he walked through. He walked right past the guards, right up to the Yellows.

"We need for you to return to your cells for the night," he said, hands clasped behind his back. "I will not ask you again."

There was this air about him—he reeked of true authority. For me, it was something admirable, something intense. It clearly wasn't coming across the way for the Yellows.

"Fuck you" was the most screamed thing, I'm sure. There were other mixes, like "you gray-haired bitch" and "you dumb cunt", but pretty much everyone yelled "fuck you" at some point.

I didn't know what the Old Man was going to do. He stood there, letting them yell. When they quieted down, he turned his head ever so slightly, and over his shoulder, said, "Don't feed them. Three days."

No yelling this time.

He turned back to them. "I will not ask you again." He turned around and walked towards us, nodding as he passed us. The guards were close enough now that they started to grab kids, throwing them to the floor, and handcuffing them. No one really fought back. No one jumped the guards, no one threw a punch. They let the guards take them down and handcuff them.

"He just broke thirty kids with five words," Socks said in awe.

"Even the dumbest of fuckers know they gotta eat," Pittman said. "You good here, Red?"

"Yeah," I said, watching the guards collect handcuffed Yellows. "I'm good."

A guard came to my cell after we had all been locked up again for the night. My back was to the door, but I could hear his boots as he walked, and I could feel him looking at me. I had always thought that people were crazy when they said they could feel someone looking at them. A few months in the prison and I knew exactly what they meant.

"Hey," he said, softly. I rolled over to look at him. "The Warden wants to see you."

I sat up as he opened the cell door. So that was the Old Man's title. I didn't know why that hadn't occurred to me sooner. "Why?" I asked.

"Just come on," the guard said. I stood up and walked over to him, and he took me by my arm and led me. We went through a few locked doors and past other guards. I was starting to get a feel for the layout of the prison. A lot of long hallways, a lot of locked doors, a lot of guards.

We got to the Warden's office. It wasn't anything special. His door didn't have one of the fancy electronic locks, but it did have a blurred glass window. No name on it, though. The guard knocked, then opened the door and nudged me inside.

The Warden was at his desk, writing on some papers. He looked up as I came in. "Hello, Heather," he said. His voice was flat, emotionless. There wasn't anything special about his office. A plain wooden desk. Some filing cabinets. A plain white mug. Nothing personal about it.

"Sit, please," he said, gesturing to one of the chairs across from him. I looked around for a second longer, then sat. His mouth scrunched up like he was trying to smile.

"I understand you were one of the leaders, back at the other prison," he said, folding his hands out in front of him.

"No," I corrected. "I was a second."

"Meaning?"

"I was Delany's number two," I said, looking at him. He didn't have a nameplate on his desk, either. "What's your name?"

"People here call me the Warden. Can I ask you something?"

"I bet your mother didn't name you that." We looked at each other for a few seconds before he sighed and leaned back in his chair.

"I read in your file that you were timid," he said, resting his clasped hands on his stomach. "I guess that's changed." I didn't say anything. I had no idea we had files, but I knew right then and there that I was going to get my hands on mine.

"How did all of this happen, Heather?"

"How did what happen?"

"The prison you were at," he said, "What is its history? How did that place come to be?"

I shook my head. "I don't know. I was only there for a few months."

"Surely Delany told you something about it. She was there for years. Her mother was there for years," he said, looking me over. I didn't like the way his eyes felt on me. He was searching for something, I just wasn't sure what it was.

"No idea," I said with a little shrug. "Delany didn't talk about it much."

"What did she talk about?"

"Why do you want to know?"

One side of his mouth curled up. "You're worried about your friend, or, I'm sorry, girlfriend?"

"Friend."

"Right. You're worried about your friend, I understand that. You should know that I meant what I said about taking care of you all. Delany is the only person here that has never been anywhere else but the prison she was born in. We want to make sure she is okay, mentally and physically. My guards told me you went into her cell to look after her. How is she adjusting?" He leaned forward when he finished taking, picking up his pen.

Something about him made my skin crawl. "She's fine," I lied. "She's upset about those we lost."

"And who did she lose?"

"A few people."

He leaned back again. "Do you trust me?" he asked.

"No."

The Warden nodded a little. "Can you do something for me? Just a little favor. We need to confirm a few things about that prison, for the record. We didn't have guards there, you see, so we have to ask. I know that might be hard for you."

"To talk about it?" I asked, almost laughing. "No, I'm fine."

He nodded again. "Alright," he picked up a pen and looked at me. "Who was in charge?"

"Well, of the groups, a few different people. But Delany was pretty much in charge. They—we all respected her. She didn't always get her way, but most of the time."

"And the groups?"

"Yeah, Red, Orange, Yellow, Green, Blue, Purple, and Pink. Though Pink really doesn't matter," I said. I looked around his office again. He might have well had just walked in as well. It looked brand new.

"And the leaders of those groups?"

"Delany is the leader of Red, I'm her second. Noel was in charge of Orange, she never picked a second. Which, neither did Cye, but that's not important. Yellow—"

"I'm sorry," he said, cutting me off. "Cye?"

"Oh, I never met her. She led Orange before I got there. Rabbit killed her," I said. The Warden's mouth opened for a second. I would have liked to take it for shock, but I don't think it was.

"Why did he kill her?"

I shrugged. "Honestly, a lot of shit happened at that prison. You just have to let some of it go." I stopped and looked at him. "Why does it matter who the leaders were?"

"It doesn't, really," the Warden said, putting his pen down for a second. "We just want to understand what happened there. As best we can."

I didn't see any harm in telling him the leaders. Most of them were dead, apparently. "Rabbit is the leader Yellow. He apparently had a second, but I never met the kid. I honestly don't think he was a real person. Brock is Green. He had a second too, a really short girl. She didn't go to meetings, so I don't really know her. Her name is Cassidy. She didn't do anything, actually. He died, right before we got picked up. Freddie leads Blue. Then there's Rue, who died as well, they led Purple."

"There were a lot of leaders," The Warden commented, quickly writing down everything I said.

"Not really. They were all supposed to have seconds, but most of them didn't," I said, shaking my head a little. The Warden looked up at me.

"Why is that, do you think?"

"Hard to trust people in a prison like that," I said. "Seconds get a lot of clout without a lot of responsibility. People fight over stuff like that."

"You had a lot of responsibility," the Warden said.

"Red is different. We're the biggest, Delany needs a second. Just in case," I said.

"Just in case she died," the Warden clarified. "Was no one else worried about dying?"

I shook my head. "No, no, no one else was worried about what would happen after they died. Delany, she cares. A lot. It mattered to her, what happened there."

The Warden wrote something down, and I regretting saying that. I don't know why I said it. I wanted him to understand, but he still skeeved me out. "And then Pink," I continued. "Taver was their leader, but there were like, twenty of them, so he didn't do much but drink all day. Pittman is pretty much in charge."

"Why were there so few in Pink?" the Warden asked.

"Pink was the only color who recruited, everyone else got assigned. If you were big and tough, Pink asked you to join. They were like, hired guns. Protected the gardens, broke up fights at the well, that sort of thing."

"And Taver, he made his own alcohol?"

"More or less," I said, thinking about it. "I never had any. I knew he had a guard connection, but I think he kept that for himself and sold the shitty stuff he made."

The Warden looked like he had just been electrocuted. "A guard connection?"

I stopped for a second. Maybe I shouldn't have said that. Why did I keep saying stuff like that? "Ugh, yeah."

"You had guards bringing you things?"

I didn't know what to say. "Taver did, yeah. Not me."

"Anyone else?"

I shook my head. "No."

"How did he—"

"I don't know," I said quickly.

The Warden looked me over for a second. Clearly, we both knew I said something I shouldn't have. He grunted a little. "Very well. Maybe we can talk about this when you've spent some time here, and feel more comfortable."

I wanted to tell him good luck with that, but I just stood up and went to the door. Hand on the doorknob, I turned to look at him. "Yellow will be easier once Rabbit is back," I said. "They are tense without him." I wanted to say that they were tense without his drugs, but I had already said enough.

"It takes people time to adjust," the Warden agreed.

I opened the door and the same guard was waiting. He took me back to my cell, wordlessly.

The guard's boots clicked away, and Pittman whispered my name. I went over to the bars and whispered back, "yeah?"

"What did they want?"

"He asked questions about the prison, and Delany" I whispered back.

"What did you tell him?"

"Nothing."

"Good."

That night, all I could dream of was Rue. How their blood gushed from their neck, how they looked, eyes wide, in shock, at the rest of us. How the blood flowed so quickly from their neck, like a river. Their purple clothes, becoming bright red. It was like Delany had claimed them as one of hers. No, like *I* had claimed them.

I woke up a few times during the night, but every time I went back to bed, it was Rue. I didn't know if they were truly a bad person. I guess they did get a sick kind of joy out of burning people, but so did pretty much everyone.

I wondered if their death made me a murder. Man-slaughter-er? I didn't get them killed on purpose. We were playing chicken; I won. *No, not me*, I thought. The ceiling above my bed was uninteresting and cold. I missed Delany's shambled roof.

They were playing with Delany. They thought she cared too much to risk everyone's lives. She cared about the whole prison. That's what they were counting on. But she trusted me. And I got people killed.

I tried to go back to sleep, but Rue haunted my dreams.

◆

Over the next two weeks, we adjusted. We woke up at seven in the morning, when they turned the lights on. We ate breakfast at seven fifteen, went outside until nine, milled around the common room until noon, had lunch until one, went back outside until two, had classes until five, dinner at five thirty, then back into the common room until nine. We were back in the cells at nine fifteen, and lights out was at ten. Like clockwork, every single day.

There were a few people that had a tough time adjusting. A Yellow, some skinny girl named Amy, who I had maybe seen once or twice before, jumped on the guards back and tried to choke him. She was tackled and taken away. We were told she was in solitary confinement.

Two other kids got into a fight, and they got taken away too. That was it, though. We still stuck to our people; Reds with Reds, Blues with Blues. We did comingle a little more, and for classes, when they divided us up based on our schooling level, everyone got a little tenser.

The guards were nice. Never said a word to us, were never rougher than they had to be. I had heard about abuse in prisons before, about beatings and rapes and stealing. We didn't have any of that. The food was subpar, but compared to eating moldy bread and rotten tomatoes, no one complained. We even started putting on weight.

We all went to the doctor, as the Warden promised. I had heard that someone people had to be tied down, but I did my exam, chatted with the doctor. She didn't say much, just asked me about my diet, if I had any sexual contact, if I was feeling okay. Normal doctor stuff.

"Is my friend, Rabbit okay?" I asked, and she frowned. "Jack," I said. "I don't know his last name."

She stepped over to a few of her files on the counter. "Do you know his ID number?"

I thought for a second. "It ends with sixty-nine," I said, trying to remember. "He used to joke about it. I don't think I remember the rest of it."

"Jack," she mumbled to herself. "Jack Pidone?"

"I guess," I said. She pulled the file out of the stack and looked at it. "Yes, he's doing alright. He should be released to you today. Released to his cell, I mean." She looked up at me and smiled. "You know, a lot of people talk about you."

"Really?" I said.

"They keep telling me how you got them here." She was a pretty woman, brown hair twisted in a bun, soft brown eyes. She was maybe in her forties. Something about her was very calming. "They sound grateful."

"I didn't do anything special," I said, "I got four people killed."

"You saved three hundred. Three hundred and eighty-two, actually" the doctor added. "That counts for something."

"I didn't save anyone. We were just fine before," I snapped. I don't know why that upset me. If anything, I had saved them from the situation I got them into. I don't think that evened out. "Are we done?" I asked, a little softer. The doctor nodded and opened the door for me.

She did tell the truth. Rabbit reappeared at the end of the day, right before we went back to our cells. People crowded around him in the common room, asking him all kinds of questions. He looked at me when he said he almost died.

"You got us into one sick place, Heather," he said, spitting as he spoke.

"You're alive, aren't you?" I asked. Delany still refused to leave her cell, no matter what they did or said. I was surprised they didn't drag her out. Right then, I wished they had. If Rabbit was about to start something, I wanted her next to me.

"Barely, and no thanks to you," he snapped.

"I told them to get a doctor for you," I said, crossing my arms. I heard Sock, somewhere behind me, confirm it.

"See?"

"That doctor almost killed me," Rabbit snapped. "Tried to shove a knife in my throat." He jabbed at his throat with his hand, to show everyone.

"What did you do, fight her off?" Someone asked. I couldn't tell if they were making fun of him or not.

"Yeah," he said, nodding. "Kicked her right in the head."

"You were probably choking on your own vomit," Freddie said, next to Rabbit. I hadn't noticed her before. "Whatever happened, you're here and that doctor doesn't look worse for wear."

Rabbit mumbled something and looked at me. "We have some shit to talk about, Red."

"Fine," I said, uncrossing my arms. "What do you want to talk about?"

Rabbit looked around. Almost all three hundred and eighty-two people were looking at us, guards included.

"Tomorrow," he said, sternly. "We got some problems."

Rabbit stomped off. I watched him for a second, waiting for everyone else to leave too. I didn't want everyone to see me running off to Delany's cell. I think Pittman noticed, or maybe he was just sick of looking at us, because he started barking for people to get moving.

"Delany," I said as I ducked into her cell. We were going to have to go to our cells for the night soon, and I had to talk to her. "Rabbit is causing problems."

She was laying on her stomach, tracing circles into her sheets. "What else is new?"

"He's going to convince people I did this to us," I said, sitting on the edge of her cot. She didn't move. "Delany," I whined.

"What? You did."

"That's not helpful."

"Neither is you being here."

She turned her head to look at me. "I had an open sky before, miles of land. Now I have this wall—" she paused to smack it with her palm, "—and someone else telling me when it's day and night."

"They let us outside," I countered. "And you could eat, if you ever left this cell."

"I was a *leader* before."

"You could be one now."

She didn't say anything for a while, just traced more circles. I watched her for a while, until the guards started calling out for people to go back to their cells. I opened my mouth to tell her goodnight when she spoke.

"When did I ever tell you when you had to go to sleep?"

I got up and left her alone with her circles.

Part Two

"Red."

Rabbit was behind me. I had been sitting at a table, talking to Socks about school. Turns out, we lived only a few miles apart, and he knew a few people that went to high school with me. Honestly, it was a much more interesting conversation than whatever Rabbit had to say.

"Hey," I said to Socks, "Give me a minute?" It occurred to me that at the old prison, I would have been worried. Worried about a fight, a weapon. Even though it was only Rabbit. Here, there was only so much damage he could do.

Socks nodded and took off. I saw him wander in the direction of Freddie and her group. I turned to look at Rabbit. "Yeah?" I asked. I was trying to be nonchalant, acting like this was a minor disturbance in my day. Rabbit didn't seem to care.

He sat down on the table, making himself taller than me. "The fuck?" he asked, just like that. No actual question, just *the fuck*.

"I didn't know this was going to happen," I said, and I was being honest. I think that confused Rabbit. Honesty was not something we dealt with often. "I thought Rue would cave way before the infected even got close to breaking out. I thought they would be worried about a riot, you guys would all cave, Delany and Noel would burn the infected, we would all move on."

"So you decided to play chicken with a bunch of criminals that have little to no sense of self-preservation? You fucked us," Rabbit said. "Are you even sorry?" He looked so genuine, more so than I had ever seen him before. I wasn't sure if it was because he was sober, or genuinely upset. Probably both.

I looked around. Everyone around me had shoes, clean clothes. No one was too cold, or too hot. No one, apart from Delany, who refused to eat any food she didn't recognize, was hungry. No one was fighting. No one was thirsty. "You know what," I said to Rabbit, a little too loud, "fuck you."

Rabbit stood up, and I did as well. "You are a lying ass drug-dealer who couldn't make a profit because you were too busy using your own product. Your people were too high to do shit all day, and your sorry ass is upset that I gave them everything you couldn't. So excuse me for feeding us, for housing us, for getting us clean water. Fuck you, you know? *Fuck you.*"

I hadn't realized how loud I was. The room had quieted down to listen to me. I could feel my heart racing in my chest, so loud it was the only thing I could hear.

Rabbit nodded a few times. Nodded wasn't the right word. Twitched. "I knew you didn't get it. This place is a trap and we all fucking know it." He tapped two fingers against my chest. "Except for you. Because you aren't one of us. And apparently, you never will be."

A guard had walked over to us, stopping about four feet away, but he let Rabbit storm off. He looked at me and I shook my head. The guard slunk back to where ever he had been standing before. I sat back down, and slowly, the room went back to whatever it was doing before.

Pittman walked over to me right away. "Hey," he said, sitting down across from me. "That was intense." I looked up at him, and I didn't even have to ask. "Rabbit has a point. You haven't been in a place like this before. We have." I wasn't sure if Rabbit had talked to him, or if this place was losing its charm.

"Isn't this place better than those?"

Pittman took in a deep breath, then let it out. "Here, we have no freedom. Every second of our day is micromanaged. There, sure. We were hungry, pissed off, half dead, and high as fuck. But no one told us what to do. People like Rabbit, people like me, we need that. We don't—we can't do the nine to five thing, you know? We handle that kind of stuff."

"George likes it here," I said.

Pittman nodded. "He does," he said. "I tried to, you know. I did. It was great, at first. I just— I can't do this sort of thing. We're not made for it."

I thought about what he said. "So you really think I fucked us?"

Pittman nodded. "You fucked me, and Rabbit, and a handful of other guys. But for you and Socks. Freddie, George, and everyone else, you saved them. It's a matter of perspective."

"So, what do I do now?" I asked. Pittman stood up.

"Unfuck us," he said with a halfhearted shrug. "Whatever that fucking means."

I sat across from the Warden. "Can I really trust you?" I asked. He was leaning back in his chair, casually. Or as casually as he could. He had on a gray suit today; it matched the streaks in his hair.

"Of course."

"Some people are unhappy here."

"You?"

"No."

The Warden leaned forward. "Rabbit, then? I heard about your fight."

I shook my head a little. "It wasn't a fight. We—they— " I stopped myself, then restarted. "Okay. We used to have a system. It wasn't perfect, but it worked. There was a certain kind of freedom." The Warden nodded. "And so, some people feel like this is worse because we lost that."

"So they don't like the oversight?"

"No."

The Warden nodded again. "Okay. And you understand why I have guards here, correct?"

"Yes."

"And you understand that that is not going to change?"

"Yes."

"Then why are you telling me this?"

I took a breath in. "I don't want a schedule. I want us to be allowed to control our own day, fully." The Warden put a hand to his chin and thought. He cocked his head to one side, then the other. His eyes moved as if he was doing math in his head. It took a good couple of minutes, but I didn't mind. He was very expressive.

"Alright," he said, finally. "We can do away with the schedule."

Everyone knew it was me. The lack of a schedule seemed to calm everyone down, with the exception of Rabbit. He was still furious, refused to look at me. I guess Delany was still mad at me too, but she still had refused to leave her cell, so the change didn't impact her at all.

I leaned against her wall, telling her about my day. She traced circles onto the wall. I had no idea if she was listening to me or not.

Rabbit marched himself into her cell and looked at the two of us. "Really?" he asked me. "This is supposed to make this place better?"

"You haven't come to see me," Delany said, letting her hand fall away from the wall. Rabbit looked at her, then back at me.

"This isn't any better," he snapped.

"I'm talking to you," Delany said, more forcefully. She would barely acknowledge when I was in the room, but Rabbit got old-school Delany. I was instantly jealous. "Why haven't you come to see me?"

"I've been busy," Rabbit snapped.

"And you don't think you need help?"

That seemed to get Rabbit's interest, and I could feel the energy in the room change. I felt like I was spying on them, though I was in the room. Neither of them were paying any attention to me now. "What do you mean?" he asked.

"I want out just as much as you do," she said. Her head cocked to the side a little, like she did when she was trying to be nice. "I was the leader of the Red, I know everyone we have here. You don't think that would be useful?"

"I know everyone too," Rabbit said, almost defensively.

"They liked you because you gave them drugs," Delany said, flat. Her head was straight again. "They *respect* me."

"You're a part of the reason we're here," Rabbit reminded her.

"And I'm the only way we'll get out," Delany finished. "Besides, Heather and Noel got us here. I had nothing to do with that."

"That's a lie," I said. No one even looked at me.

"Twist it a little," Delany explained. "With everything that happened, no one will remember exactly what happened. Besides, I didn't come up with the plan. That's the truth."

"I feel like that's a pretty big thing for them to forget," Rabbit said, crossing his arms.

Delany was into it now, putting on a show. "No, I wasn't even at the burning, I was busy trying to rebuild our home. It was Heather and Noel, they did all of it. I wasn't there," she chirped.

"People connect you with Heather so much, we can convince them that they saw her and assumed you were there too," Rabbit said, nodding. "Alright. What's your plan to get out?"

Delany leaned back, away from him. Her hand went back to the wall, tracing more circles. "I'm working on that."

Rabbit told her to hurry, looked at me, then left.

"Delany—"

"Get out."

"Delany, you know that's not going to work."

"Get out."

◆

It worked.

It only took a few days for people to start whispering that I was the cause for everything. Noel, being dead, was totally blameless. Delany, who convinced everyone she had no part in this, was also blameless. And then there was me.

Though, it wasn't entirely a bad rumor. Those who could see what we had gained in the move thought even higher of me. I had people asking me to sit with them at lunch, to hang out with me in the courtyard. It was kind of nice. But whatever rift moving had created between us, it only got worse with the new rumor.

Red was with Delany, blindly. It didn't matter what she said; they knew where she was, they didn't care if she lied about it. Yellow was with her as well. They also managed to grab most of Green and Purple. That left me with Orange, Blue, and Pink. We were vastly outnumbered.

Freddie stood next to me in the courtyard, watching everyone. There were a few odd people who didn't stick with their colors, but those people were few and far between. "So, what, they are going to plan an escape? Try to go back?" Freddie asked me.

"I don't know," I said, watching Rabbit and Delany talk. Whatever was being said, they both laughed.

"Can you talk to the Warden?" Socks asked me. "He likes you."

"I don't think that is helping our cause at all," Freddie said.

"If we tell him they are going to escape, he might be able to stop them," Socks added. They were quiet, and I realized they were both looking at me.

"Oh. Yeah, I could try. He hasn't asked for me in a while," I said, still watching Delany and Rabbit. They were moving their hands around as they spoke. Delany had just started leaving her cell this morning, and only with Rabbit at her side. He walked her everywhere. I bit my bottom lip for a second.

It took a whole week for the Warden to call for me. When he did, it was out in front of everyone. A guard came and told me, then led me by my arm out of the common room. I couldn't see Delany and Rabbit and their bunch as I walked away, but I could feel them looking at me.

I sat down across from the Warden. I was getting comfortable in his office, now. The empty walls didn't freak me out, his blank expression didn't set off any red flags. "Hey," I said, as I let myself fall into the chair. "What's going on?"

"I was going to ask you that," he said, and under his beard, I saw a bit of a smile.

I debated telling him all of it, but I didn't know what would happen to Delany and Rabbit and the rest of them. "They are still unhappy."

"Everyone?"

"No."

"Just the people who spend time with Delany and Jack."

"Jack? Oh, Rabbit, yeah. Yeah, they aren't happy."

"Why not?"

I didn't know how to word it. "They want their freedom back. Still," I said, cautiously. I didn't know what answer the Warden had been expecting, but this wasn't it.

"Back? Back how? They were in a prison before." He leaned forward, though I don't know if he was angry or just confused.

I started slowly. "They had—well, freedom. No one told them what to do, no one—"

"I let them make their own schedule."

It was anger, then. Part of me was annoyed with him, for being angry. But part of me understood it. He had done what he could to make everyone comfortable here, and it still wasn't enough. I nodded. "Yeah, but there are still guards. There are still cells. There are still lights out. Before, we had parties in the middle of the night. We had gross, home-made alcohol and they managed to sneak in drugs. We had fist fights and dances and I—" I realized now even I was longing for it, the old prison. I took a second to focus.

"They miss those things," I said. "They miss them more than they want food or a roof."

The Warden leaned back in his chair, and it squeaked. He put a hand to his chin. He didn't say anything for a little while. "Heather," he said. I had forgotten he knew my name. "I was thinking of something, but it would take a lot of work and negotiation, and I don't want to make any moves unless I knew it would help." I waited for him to keep talking. "There was an old prison not too far from here, it was more outdoors, more open. Do you think they would like it there?"

I knew the answer before he had finished the question. No. They wanted their freedom, they wouldn't be happy anywhere with a warden, even with one who was trying to help them.

"What's it like there?" I asked. I was fishing, and he knew it. I didn't want to break out because I didn't know what would happen. Delany and Rabbit didn't care about that risk; to them, it was worth it. But if I could get us an outdoor prison, something more open, something with less security, I could boost the chances of them getting out safely.

"It has a few small houses, enough to fit everyone four to a house. The houses aren't connected, but there are still all of the comforts we have here. There's a large fence, like the one you were used to," he spoke, studying me. I knew he was trying to figure out my angle.

"Is it electric? The fence?"

"No."

"It needs to be."

He nodded. I think that satisfied him. I needed him to trust me, to think that I was on his side. Because I was. Mostly.

"I'll see what I can do to get us there. Don't say anything to anyone, please."

◆

"Heather."

It was Delany. I rolled over and blinked a few times, trying to clear my eyes. It was dark—the hallway had dimmed lights, but they weren't much use. I could see her outline, next to Rabbits. "How did you guys get over here?" I whispered.

Rabbit held up something, but I couldn't tell what it was. "Come here," he said. I stood up, rubbing my eyes, and went over to the bars.

"Sucks to be in there when we're out here, huh?" Rabbit teased. No one paid attention to him.

"I want you on our side with this," Delany said in a low whisper. It reminded me of when she would talk in her sleep at the old prison. It wasn't often, but it was always in the same low, husky tone.

"What happens if you guys fail?" I asked them. "There are prisons much worse than this."

"Yeah, we were at it," Rabbit said. "That's how half of us got there in the first place." He couldn't see the look I was giving him. "Delany, do your thing."

Delany sighed. "Heather, listen," she said, softly. "We are going to do this with or without you. Jose went missing yesterday. No one has seen him. Something weird is going on here."

It took me a second to remember who Jose was. He was at the party where Rabbit gave me drugs, or at least I thought he was. "Have you asked the guards?" I asked.

"They said he would be 'back shortly', that's it," Delany said. Her voice was pleading this time. "We have to get out of here."

"So we can what, starve to death?" I asked.

Rabbit clicked his teeth. "Listen, we've had three people starve to death out of like seven hundred something. So far, I've been carted off, and Jose is missing. He's a good kid, Heather."

"They brought you back," I pointed out.

"Look, give it a week. If Jose comes back, I'll reconsider," Delany said, and Rabbit groaned. "If he doesn't, you'll give us a chance. Deal?"

"Deal."

Delany and Rabbit strolled up to me. It had been seven days. "Socks, can I have a minute," I asked as they got closer. He followed my gaze and sighed.

"Don't get caught up in their shit. We get the chess board in like twenty minutes," he said before slinking off.

Delany and Rabbit stopped in front of me. Rabbit looked all too smug. "It's been a week," he said.

"I know."

"And?" Delany asked.

I had asked around. Jose had, in fact, gone missing. The guards told me the same line they told Delany. The Warden hadn't called for me. My best bet was that they took him. I sighed. "Alright, yeah, something is weird about that."

"So you'll consider it? Working with us?" Delany asked. I had never heard her ask anything with this tone, it was almost pleading.

For a second, a look flashed over her face. The same look after she burned people. It wasn't anger, it was pure terror. She was terrified I would say no.

"Delany, I—"

She cut me off. "No more bullshit. Rabbit is useless, I have no idea what I'm doing. You know this place, you know this world. We need you." She didn't look scared anymore. It occurred to me that Delany was probably the strongest person I have ever met.

"Yeah," I said. "Yeah, I'll help."

I had no idea why I said it. It hurt to even say. Unlike with the last plan we had constructed, I *knew* this was going to get people killed. It was this sinking feeling in my gut, a definitive feeling that I was doing the wrong thing. But Delany and Rabbit were going to get themselves killed. The least I could do was minimize the risk.

◆

I woke up to the soft clink of metal on metal. I could see two outlines; Delany and Rabbit. Rabbit picked the lock to my cell door, slid it open, and stepped inside.

"Considering I haven't done that in like, seven years, I'm pretty good at this shit," he said with a smile.

"Seven years ago, you were eleven," Delany whispered. "Shut up."

I had no idea if her math was right or not, but I was impressed with her either way.

"That makes it even more impressive, idiot," Rabbit said. He sat on the edge of my sink, and I swear I could see it bow under his weight. I sat up in the bed so Delany could sit next to me.

"What's the plan?" I whispered.

Delany looked at me. "Well, we were hoping you would help with the finer points of it," she mumbled and looked at Rabbit.

"The riot that got me and Pitt thrown into the other prison, four people died," he said, a little too loudly. A few cells over, someone coughed.

"Four prisoners, or guards?" I asked.

He hesitated for a second, looking up at the ceiling. "Three of us. One of them," Rabbit answered. "If we can get something that wild going again, we might be able to make an escape."

"An escape for *everyone*? All three hundred and eighty-two of us?" I asked, looking between the both of them. "We'd have to kill all of the guards to get that done."

Rabbit shrugged one shoulder, as if that was something he had already considered. Delany rolled her eyes. "No, just those who want to go," she said.

"So, let's say one hundred and eighty," I guessed. "You want one hundred and eighty people to just waltz out of a prison."

"Yeah," Delany said with a little nod. "I do." Delany meant it to. I knew she did.

I sighed. I didn't know if I should tell them about the possibility of moving to a new prison. They might be willing to wait or they might want to try to escape even sooner. I had no idea what they would do with that information, or if they would spread it around or not. If only I wasn't dealing with unstable criminals. "What's the plan so far? Just a riot?" I asked

Rabbit pushed off of the sink. "So. We need everyone outside, in that fenced in space—"

"We couldn't fit a hundred people there, let alone—"

"Once we do that, we jam the door, scale the fence, kill those two guards, and bolt," Rabbit said, not letting me speak. "Done deal."

"There's more than one exit," I said, my voice flat. "You realize that, right? They would go to another exit." Neither of them said anything. "And those two guards have guns."

"Pittman told us they are—I don't fucking remember, some kind of gun that takes a while to reload. That's two shots, then we have time," Delany said. "It could work."

Delany had never seen a gun before now, never heard one being fired, never seen the damage it could do. "Alright," I said calmly. "Let me think it over and see what I can come up with."

They left me alone for about four days. Delany had retreated back to her cell; I don't know what it was that scared her this time, but she was back in there again, and she wasn't leaving. Rabbit was bouncing around again, talking to everyone he could. I didn't know if he found a way to get more drugs, or if he was just excited to go home.

Home. It still felt weird to me. When I thought of home, I thought of Delany's little shack, the cages scarred with burnt flesh, the little gardens the Green's had, with their strawberries the size of your pinky nail. That felt like home.

I didn't have a bad home life before, or an abusive mother or anything. Everything was fine. I had friends, I did well in school. It was fine. Fine. Only fine, nothing more, nothing less. The prison, the first prison, was exciting. It was hot and sticky, it was loud, and it was home. Walking around in the grass field, waiting in line to drink from a dirty well, walking through the rain, listening to someone play homemade drums—I don't know if it was a sense of community I had been lacking before, or I was lonely, or what, but that shithole was home.

My chest ached as I thought about it. I wanted to go back, too. I don't know if I wanted it so bad I would risk dying for it, though. Hell, no one had any idea where we were. We could be ten feet from it, or a thousand miles.

Next to me, Freddie coughed. "I think I'm getting sick," she said, pulling me out of my thoughts. "Cassidy, that annoying Green girl, she was coughing all last night."

I stood up and moved in front of her. "Stick out your tongue," I said, and she did. I looked at her throat. I pulled away, and she closed her mouth.

"What?" she asked as I put my hand on her forehead.

"You need to see the doctor," I said. "You're burning up and your throat is all red."

"I'm Blue," Freddie joked. "I'll see her after lunch."

"Go now," I said, and Freddie looked at me for a second. "Please," I said, trying to soften it. "You could get other people sick."

"Fine, fine," she said standing up and slinking past me. "Such a worry wart, Red."

◆

Rabbit wandered up to me while I was eating lunch. It was some kind of meat sandwich and slightly brown apple slices. I was saving the apples for Delany. I thought maybe I could talk her into trying one. She liked strawberries. Apples were close enough.

"Hey," he said and sat down across from me. One of his hands reached out and grabbed an apple slice, tossing it into his mouth.

"I'm not sharing this meal three ways," I said, pulling my tray a little closer to me.

"Where's your new boyfriend?" Rabbit asked, looking around. "Socks," he said when I didn't say anything. "Also, you're welcome for not making a threesome joke right there."

"Not my boyfriend," I corrected. "And he's mad at me."

"Why?"

"You."

"Me?"

I looked at Rabbit for a second. "Yeah, that's fair," he admitted with a smile. "Socks isn't like me."

"I think you mean *doesn't like you*," I said.

"No, he *isn't* like me," Rabbit insisted. "Listen, you got you guys, who are good kids who did something fucked, right? Accidentally ran someone over, stole some jewelry to impress your friends, shit like that. Then there are people like me, who are fucked up. You did something fucked, I am fucked. There's a difference."

I nodded. "Pitt told me the same thing."

Rabbit reached across and took some more of my eggs. "Because Pitt is also fucked up. The fucked up bunch of us, we aren't meant for a place like this. You and Socks are."

He stood up. "That's why we gotta get *us* away from *you*."

I brought the apples into Delany's cell after lunch. She didn't look up at me. "Delany," I said, sitting down on the edge of her cot. "Delany?" I went and stroked her hair. She let me touch her more and more the last few days, like an animal too tired to fight anymore. "I brought you some apples."

I could hear her shallow breaths, but she didn't answer me.

"Delany?" I said, pushing her hair away from her face. Her eyes were starting to look yellow. She smelled like sweat and piss. "Delany, we gotta do something with you, come on." She didn't move. "Get up," I practically yelled. "I'm sick of this shit. You have to do something." She didn't move.

I put the apples down next to her and left. I found Pitt in the common room almost instantly—he was still the tallest of us. "I need your help," I said sternly.

"With what?" he asked, shuffling a deck of cards.

"Delany."

"She alright?"

"No."

He followed me back to her cell without hesitating. "Aw, fuck," he said when he saw her. "She's going to die."

"What do you mean?" I snapped. "She's fine, she just needs a shower."

"No," Pittman said. "This place is going to kill her."

"No." This time it was an order. "Pick her up, we're taking her to the showers."

Pittman didn't seem convinced, but he did as I asked. He carried her with ease—she was even thinner than she used to be. I hadn't seen her eat anything in about four days. Pittman carried her out of the cell, and two guards came running at us.

"Put her down!" one of them ordered. I got between Pittman and the guards.

"Listen, she needs help. From us. Tell the Warden I'll take care of it," I said, putting two hands up, as if surrendering. "He'll trust me."

One of the grabbed the walkie-talkie on his chest and mumbled into it. Someone on the other end mumbled back.

"He said fine," the guard said. They were both eyeing us. "But she has to see a doctor afterward."

"Deal," I said.

Pittman and I walked to the showers. He held her while I turned it on, waiting for it to heat up. "She'll be fine after a good shower," I insisted. "Help me get her clothes off."

"Oh, wow," Pittman said, looking at me like I had grown another head, "*No.*"

"Pitt, I can't hold her up and undress her. She'll deadweight on me," I said. "She's barely conscious, just help me."

"If she starts fighting us, you're on your own," Pittman warned. He helped me hold her up and undress her. She flopped around like a rag doll.

"She's dehydrated," Pittman said. "Does she know how the sink works?"

"I showed her," I said as I struggled to get her pants off from around her limp foot.

"Has she actually been drinking though?" he asked.

"I don't know, Pitt, I've got other shit going on right now," I snapped. I pulled at her pants, and her ankle made a little popping noise as I pulled. "Let's just get her in there."

Pittman refused to hold her in the shower, so I did. Soaking my clothes, I had to hold her up by one arm and lean her against the stall door to keep her upright. "Delany, come on," I said. She was barely holding her head up anymore. "I know part of this is an act. I need you to get it together. I can't take care of everyone and you."

I was practically begging her. We stood in the shower for maybe five minutes together. "Pitt," I said, struggling as one of her legs started to give out. "Go get help. We're going to need a stretcher."

They came rushing into the bathroom in maybe sixty seconds. One of the nurses and the pretty doctor helped me get her onto the stretcher and covered with a blanket.

"She's given up," I told them. "She can't stay here."

The nurse rushed her back out of the bathroom. The doctor took my hand. "Does she have any medical conditions?" she asked me. She looked genuinely concerned.

"She's been malnourished her whole life," I said, "lice, fleas, skin rashes, that whole thing. I don't know of anything specific." I stopped talking and the doctor turned to go, so I grabbed her hand back. "She needs an IV, probably a feeding tube," I said. "Listen, you have to sedate her. If she wakes up with all of that attached to her, she'll kill herself to get it off. I'm not kidding. She has no idea what a needle is."

The doctor nodded. "You did the right thing," she told me before she rushed off.

I looked up at Pittman, pathetic and soaking wet. When I had taken Rabbit's drugs, I was out for about a day and a half. Delany got me home, herself. She made sure I was on my side, in case I threw up. She had Byrdie watch me. She stayed close by. She made sure I was okay.

When Delany needed me, I struggled. I couldn't fix her. I had to ask for help. Something salty touched my lip, and I realized I was crying.

"You know you're never going to see her again."

◆

Rabbit came by my cell right before we had to turn in for the night. I was hiding. I didn't want to see anyone after they took Delany. "Delany's gone?" he asked, hanging his arms through the cell door and resting there.

"Yeah, she wasn't eating or drinking, I had to get the doctor to take her," I said, looking up from my book. It wasn't very good anyway.

"Good," Rabbit said with one sure nod. "She was becoming deadweight."

"*Rabbit!*"

"She was," he said. "Everyone was wondering what she was thinking, what she was doing. You would have stayed here to watch her. That's not the point, remember."

"Well, if we leave, she's going too," I said. "She has to."

"See," Rabbit said, pointing a dirty finger at me. "It's thinking like that that will never get us out of here."

"Go away," I said. Rabbit smiled at me quickly, unhooked his arms, and left.

◆

I woke up coughing. "Motherfucker," I whispered to myself as I sat up. "I do not have time for this." I coughed again, then got up and took the two steps over to the sink. I ran it, put my head under, and took a sip.

It didn't help. I coughed again and again. "Freddie," I groaned. From what I could tell, lights on would be soon. I went back to my bed, trying to get comfortable. Nothing worked. I coughed for the rest of the hour, my throat burning.

The second my cell door was opened, I went towards the doctor's office. "Hey," I told the guard who was standing outside of the door. "I need to see the doctor. I have a cold."

"Colds are normal," he said. "Drink some water and rest."

I looked at him for a second. "Freddie got seen yesterday for the same thing, she's the one who got me sick. All I need is some cough medicine or something."

"I said go rest." This was the first time a guard had raised his voice at me. I crossed my arms.

"Excuse me?" I snapped. "You're going to deny me medical care? I want to speak to the Warden."

The guard moved quickly, grabbing me by both of my arms. "You'll do as I say," he snapped, starting to pull me down the hallway.

"Ow, let go! You're hurting me!" I screamed, my already sore throat burning. "Let go!"

Pittman was in the hallway still. He started to run at us. I don't think the guard realized right away, he was busy trying to hold me while I struggled. Pittman uppercutted him, knocking his head back so hard it sounded like something snapped.

He let go of me instantly, dropping straight to the floor. "Are you okay?" Pittman asked, not even looking at the guard. He was out cold. I could hear other guards running towards us. I rubbed my wrist where he had grabbed me.

"Yeah," I said, looking up at him. "You shouldn't have done that."

Pittman looked down at him. "You're welcome."

Two guards grabbed Pitt, one on each arm. He didn't fight them. A third and fourth guard followed them down the hallway. Another guard, one I had never seen before, asked me what happened. I told her the guard was hurting me, and Pittman stopped him.

"Let's get you to the Warden," she said.

"No," I ordered. "I'm going to the doctor. The Warden can see me there."

It took maybe three minutes for the Warden to show up. The nurse bounced around us, putting one of those armbands on me to check my blood pressure, getting me another pillow so I could sit up. "What's going on?" The Warden asked me, nodding towards the bed.

"I'm sick, and your guard assaulted me while I tried to get medical care," I said as the nurse asked me to open my mouth. I did and she set a thermometer in.

"I'll speak to the guards and see what happened," the Warden promised.

I held the thermometer in place while I spoke; "I just told you what happened. You need to fire him."

The Warden shook his head once. "No. I will look into this."

"Listen," I said. The nurse came over and took the thermometer out of my mouth, making a tsk sound when she did. "If my people see your guards assaulting us with no repercussions, things are going to get bad. Fast."

"I didn't say that," the Warden corrected. "I'm not firing him."

Behind us, the door swung open dramatically. Two guards, half dragging a boy, came barging in. The two nurses ran to them, helping get the boy into the nearest bed. The Warden and I both watched as the boy leaned over the side of the bed and threw up.

"We're all going to get sick," I said, mostly to myself. I wasn't even sure if the Warden heard me. "Fuck."

"Watch your language," he said, still watching the boy. He walked out of the room, the two guards trailing behind him.

Over the next six hours, nineteen more inmates were brought into the infirmary. I gave up my bed to Socks, who had also started throwing up. I sat on the floor next to him, an old mop bucket next to me in case he had to throw up again.

"This is bad, Heather," he said to me, his eyes red and glassy.

"Yeah," I said, starting to feel nauseous myself. "This is bad."

"Delany? Freddie?"

"No."

"Shit."

"Yup."

We were too weak to speak in full sentences. I hadn't seen Freddie or Delany since I had been in there. I had no idea where they were. I had tried to ask the doctor, but she told me she was busy. That was fair, though. More than half the room was throwing up.

I must have fallen asleep, because I woke up in a ball, shaking. "Here," someone said, and I felt a blanket fall around me. I shivered under it, shaking so hard my head was bouncing against the cold title.

By the third day, every single one of us was sick. Pittman had collapsed in the hallway—they couldn't move him, and had nowhere to take him, so they set him up right there.

Most people were in their cells, being seen when they could. With two nurses, one doctor, and three hundred and eighty-two of us, it wasn't often. Some of the guards would go get you water, if you asked, but I hadn't tried yet. I didn't want to speak to any of them.

I managed to get to my feet sometime in the late afternoon on the third day. I used Socks' bed, pulling half of it with me, to stand up. "You shouldn't do that," he told me, inching back away from me. "Here, lay down. I'll take the floor for a while."

"No, I'm going to see the Warden," I said, hunched over. "We gotta do something."

If Socks said anything, I couldn't hear him. I wandered out of the room and into the hallway. Pittman was laying on the floor, taking up half the hallway. "Red," he said when he saw me. "I'm going to die. Where is George?" I hadn't seen George, I figured he was in his cell, throwing up.

"No," I said, taking slow steps over to him. "No. I'm going to fix it. George is okay."

It must have taken me forty minutes to walk down the hallway. The guard who blocked the doorway just looked at me. It was the same guard from before, who had stopped me from seeing the doctor. "Please," I said, too tired to fight him. "The Warden."

He opened the door and let me through, following behind me as I walked down the next hallway. I felt like my knees were going to give out; the guard could probably hear them clanking together. It felt like another forty minutes to get to the Warden's office.

I didn't knock, I just opened the door. "We need help," I said. He was sitting at his desk, looking at a file. "You have to do something." I had to lean in the doorway to stay upright.

"I am," he said, then stopped. I went the rest of the way into the room and fell into the chair.

"We—"I had to stop to catch my breath. "We are sick. You aren't. Something is wrong."

"We have doctor's looking into why," the Warden said. "We believe there was something at Prison 917, or something here, that you hadn't been exposed to before." His words sounded far away.

"We need help *now*."

The Warden nodded. "I agree. We are moving everyone to a new prison, the one I mentioned before. It has a much bigger sick area, and a much better medical supply. We're going to start moving you tonight."

"Delany and Freddie," I said, pausing to breathe. "They go first."

The Warden nodded. "You will be on their bus."

I struggled to stand up. "No," I said. "I'm fine. Take Socks, Laura, Pittman, George, Johnny, and Forty-Eight first. Make sure Pitt and George stay together," I said, swaying as I stood. "I'm fine."

And then I fainted.

Part Three

I woke up with an IV in my arm. My eyes fluttered open and I could see the little needle taped down on my left arm. I took a breath in, and coughed. *Still sick then*, I thought. But my head felt clear, like I could think again.

I looked around the room. It was brighter than the last prison. The air smelt cleaner. There were rows and rows of beds now; way more than the fifteen we had before. There were maybe forty beds now. Every single one was taken.

I couldn't see all the way down the row to see who was who, so I got up. The IV in my arm ached as I tried to bend it, but I was able to get up and walk, one hand pulling the little IV stand with me. One of the nurses saw me and told me to go lay down.

"I feel okay," I said, "Promise. Give the bed to someone else, I can go to my cell."

The nurse put the back of her hand on my forehead. "Fine," she said, but she clearly wasn't happy about it. She took my arm and looked at the number tattooed on it. "Talk to one of the guards."

I walked down the rest of the rows of beds. Socks was there, still asleep. They had managed to get Pittman into a bed, though his feet were hanging over the edge a little. George was next to him, on his side, so he was looking at Pitt. He smiled when he saw me, but he didn't say anything. I didn't see Freddie, or Delany, or Rabbit.

The guard who was standing on the porch asked me if I was okay. "I'm fine," I said, looking around. There were trees—something we never had before. Tall, evergreen trees scattered about. I wondered how long it would take Rabbit to try to climb one.

The Warden had been right, this was a much more open prison. The housing looked like little cabins. I had never been to a camp before, but I imagine this is what it would be like. Little wooden cabins spread around. These all had bars on the doors and windows, but the aesthetic was still there.

I was going to ask the guard to get the Warden for me—I couldn't take the IV stand around on the ground with me, but he came out of one of the little cabins near us and I waved.

"I see you're doing better," he said, arms tucked behind him.

"Are we set up in housing yet?" I asked.

"No. We are working on assignments right now. I am trying to keep the groups together."

I nodded. "Good call. Where's my cell?"

The Warden looked uncomfortable for a second. "We're going to keep you here, in the infirmary, for a bit longer." I wanted to ask him why, but he chirped out a little excuse me and hurried off.

◆

We got better. It took some time, but we were getting there. After a week of being at the new prison, just about everyone was up on their feet. The Warden waited until every person was out of the infirmary before he addressed all of us.

Out in the sunlight, his hair looked more silver. Even though it was warm, he still wore a full suit. He stood on the little porch to his office, waiting for us to quiet down. It almost reminded me of the burnings, all of us gathered around outside like that. When we were mostly quiet, he spoke.

"Welcome," he said. "You are now at Prison 456. We are still unsure of what was making you all sick, but we hope to avoid similar issues in this prison. As I'm sure you realize, this prison is mostly outdoors, similar to 917. Also similar to 917 is the electric fence. Please do not touch it. We are happy to announce that there were only two casualties during the move here. Similar to your last prison, we will have scheduled events you may choose to attend."

And that was it. We went back to doing what we had before. There were classes; two of the cabins had been turned into classrooms with chairs that squeaked and chalkboards older than us. The mess hall was small and always too warm. The communal bathrooms always smelt, but no one could figure out why, or what the smell was. Everything sort of fell back into place.

Except for Rabbit. Two days out of his sick bed and he was roaming. I went to the zoo once and one of the tigers ran up and down the length of the fence, staring at us. His keeper told us he was tense, because of a storm that was supposed to be coming in a few days. He paced up and down, up and down, staring us all down. The storm never came. Rabbit stalked the fence here the same way, up and down, up and down.

And like the tiger, I watched him. He knew I was watching him, but it didn't stop him. Even the guards watched him. I followed him around for two days, nonstop.

"You could just ask him what he's planning," Freddie said, cleaning out her fingernails next to me. "He would probably tell you." Her nails clicked together.

I shook my head. "I don't think so. How's Delany?" I didn't take my eyes off of Rabbit, but the click of Freddie's nails stopped.

"She's fine," Freddie said, but she was lying. "She won't leave her room, but Laura is taking care of her."

"Laura?"

"Yeah, she's Purple. Sweet girl, makes sure she eats and whatever."

"She rooms with you guys?"

"Yeah, it's me, Laura, Delany, and George."

"Huh."

"I thought the Warden told you he was going to keep the groups together?"

I heard her, but Rabbit bent over to look at the bottom of the fence. I didn't care about the Warden. I didn't care about room assignments. Rabbit was planning something and Delany— she moved on. I expected that to hurt more, that someone else was taking care of her. That she didn't need me. She had refused to see me—not that I had much time for her at the moment. I expected a little ache in my chest, but there was nothing.

"So, why are we watching him again?" Freddie asked, and her nails started to click together again.

"To see what he's up to."

"You could just ask him."

"He'd lie."

"To you?"

"Ugh, yeah."

◆

It took me a week to figure out what he was up to. Rabbit and Pittman were sitting under a tree, whispering. I walked over and stood in front of them. "I figured it out."

Rabbit nodded. "Took you long enough."

That caught me off guard. "Do the guards know?"

Rabbit shook his head no. "You in?"

"Am I in what?" I asked, crossing my arms.

"Sit, stop lording," Pittman ordered. I uncrossed my arms and sat down.

"Are you in? For an escape?" Rabbit asked, looking me up and down.

"Listen," I said, checking around for guards quickly. "You figured out how to get past the fence. That doesn't solve the gun issue."

"Same plan as before," Rabbit said, putting both hands behind his head. "Riot."

"They'll still come after you," I told him. "And people in the riot will die."

"First of all," Rabbit said, starting to smile. "I would let every single one of you die if it meant I could walk away. Secondly, I'm very fast. *Rabbit*, remember?"

"So you're going to be a fugitive for the rest of your life? Constantly being hunted down, scared, on edge?" I asked him.

"Babe, I already am," he said, moving his arms on his knees and leaning towards me. "Listen, I'm already a fucking nut case. Two options: pretend I'm not and suffer, or acknowledge that I am and roll with it. I'm doing this with or without you."

⬣

Rabbit wasn't kidding. I was bunking with Socks, some kid named Simon, and some Green I could never remember the name of. I was half awake, the sunlight shining through the door and onto my leg, making a nice warm patch. I hunkered down, thinking of how nice it was just to lay in bed, just for a bit longer.

CRASH.

I waited a few seconds. Maybe the crash was on purpose. Maybe it was a guard or a garbage truck. Maybe I had just made it up.

No, there's yelling now.

I slowly—too slowly for the situation, as it turns out— got out of my nice warm bed and went to the door. I had barely touched it, expecting it to be locked still, but at the slight pressure from my fingertips, it swung open.

"That's not good," Socks said from his bunk. I hadn't realized he'd been watching me.

"Nope," I agreed, and walked through the door.

I didn't know that Rabbit was prepared for a riot so soon. People were running everywhere—under a tree, not fifty feet from me, a guard lay in a pool of blood. "Fucking shit," I said with the tone of an annoyed mother more so than a criminal in the mists of a riot. Looking around, there didn't seem to be any order, or mission to this riot; people were just running, screaming, breaking things. I could see people across the way opening their doors, realizing what was going on, and joining in.

If nothing else, we were good at this sort of thing. I turned and went back inside. "Socks, come on, I need you," I said, shoving my feet into my boots. "We have to find Rabbit. Simon, stay with them," I ordered, pointing to the person still in their bed. They hadn't moved at all, even with all the noise.

"What's the plan?" Socks asked as he hopped off the top bunk and shoved his boots on as well.

"We have to find Rabbit," I said, starting for the door. "Get him to call this off."

Socks got outside and looked around as well. "My bet is, he's the one who took the guard's gun," he said, pointing over to the dead body. There was an empty gun holster on his waistband.

"I haven't heard any gunshots yet," I said, "Come on, this way."

"What was that crash?" Socks asked, following behind me. We were weaving in and out of running people, some of them with pillows in their hands, some with pieces of metal.

"I'm guessing a bunk bed," I said, nodding towards a boy with a long piece of metal. "They need weapons."

We rounded a corner and saw four guards, each wrestling with a prisoner. They were trying to restrain them, but the prisoners were kicking, punching, biting, screaming; anything they could do. On the ground behind them, two people were already face down, their hands zip-tied behind their backs. Still, they were trying to wiggle away.

"Nope," I said, and turned around and started the other way.

"Where are the rest of the guards?" Socks asked, looking around. "There are usually like thirty of them, at least."

"Nightshift."

"Pitt."

I turned around, and there he was, towering over us, metal pipe in his hand. That one wasn't from a bunk though. It looked like a water pipe, maybe. He held the massive thing like a club, over one shoulder.

"You in now?" he asked. He was smiling.

"No," I snapped. "Where's Rabbit? Where's George for that matter?"

"George is with the others who didn't want to go, but don't get excited, he's coming with me. Always," he said, then used the club to point across the way.

Two guards were trying to get close to Rabbit. It looked like they were trying to talk to him. He had a gun in his hands, pointing it at whichever one of them was closest to him at that moment and then switching to the other. Every time one of them moved towards him, he pointed the gun at them until they backed up.

"Fuck, he's going to kill someone," Socks said, sounding more annoyed than horrified.

"Probably one of us," Pittman agreed.

"Come on," I said, and took off running towards Rabbit. I had no idea if the other two were following me. It didn't matter.

I ran up to them, and Rabbit smiled when he saw me. Pointing the gun at one of the guards, he laughed. "There's my girl! I knew you couldn't resist."

"No," I huffed, "I'm trying to make sure you don't kill anyone."

"Backup, inmate," one of the guards barked.

"I don't think you're in any position to give orders," I reminded him. "Rabbit, come on."

"Come on what? Either I have to shoot them or they are going to tie themselves up for me," Rabbit said. Neither of the guards said anything. "Alright then, we're at an impasse."

"No we aren't," Pittman said. I hadn't heard him walk up behind me. "Shoot them."

Rabbit shrugged. "Okay."

Both of the guards rushed him at the same time. Either Rabbit was too shocked or too scared, but either way, he didn't shoot. One guard went for the gun while the other tried to pin him down. I have no idea what came over me, maybe I was just worried for Rabbit. I grabbed one of the guards by the back of his collar and ripped him off of Rabbit. I guess he wasn't expecting that, because it was a lot easier than I thought.

Socks helped me pin him down, all the while he flailed and screamed. I took the ring of zip ties in his pocket and tied his hands together behind his back. This guard didn't have a gun on him. I hadn't even thought of the other guard, but when we were finished and I looked over, Pittman was handing the gun back to Rabbit. Their guard was lying face down in a quickly growing pool of blood. I could smell smoke, but nothing seemed to be on fire.

It had taken us maybe fifteen seconds to cuff a guard and kill a person. It happened so fast, I didn't even realize what I was doing. What *we* were doing.

"Pitt," Socks scolded.

Pittman shrugged. I noticed a second gun in his hand.

"Now what?" I snapped at Rabbit. "Give me that." I reached for the gun, and Rabbit yanked his hand back.

"No, no," he said, hopping a step back. "You can't always be in charge."

"What's your plan then?" I asked, standing up. The guard started to yell again, and I kicked him in the ribs.

Rabbit was beaming. "Now we go after the Warden."

Before I could even voice a thought about that, Delany and Laura ran by, hand in hand. "Hey!" Rabbit yelled after them. "Delany!"

She stopped, forcing Laura to stop as well. I hadn't really seen Laura before, but she was pretty. Dark brown hair, cut short like a boy's, and tall. Her legs must have been eighty percent of her body. She smiled at us, holding Delany's hand like her life depended on it.

"We're going after the Warden, you and your girlfriend want in?" he asked, shaking the gun in his hand a little. Delany let out a loud laugh.

"No, Jack," she said, looking at Laura. "We're breaking for it now, before you assholes get caught."

"Delany, I—" I started to say, but Delany's look stopped me. "Be safe," I said instead. She kissed Laura on the cheek and took off.

"Well," Socks said, "That was awkward. But back to the whole murder the Warden thing."

"No one said *murder*," Rabbit said, very innocently. "This is an *execution*. We are punishing him for his crimes." In the distance, someone started screaming bloody murder.

"Semantics," Socks countered.

"Bless you," Rabbit joked. "Come on, let's go."

Rabbit and Pittman took off running towards the Warden's office. I looked at Socks. "I do kind of want to see what our files say," I admitted.

"And stop a murder," Socks added.

"I'm a bit more on the fence about that then you would think," I said. "Come on."

By the time we got there, Rabbit and Pittman were already holding up the Warden. It would have been funny, little Rabbit next to big Pittman, pointing guns at a tired looking man who, honestly, could not have looked more relaxed.

"Hey, I want to get into our files," I said. Rabbit nodded at me to a beat, as if he suddenly heard music.

"That a girl, getting into it!" he cheered, then nodded towards the file cabinet. "Let's see what we can find."

"Heather, my dear, you—" the Warden started to say.

"Aye," Pittman barked. "No talking, dickhead." Rabbit let out a loud, long laugh, as if that was the funniest thing he had ever heard. Pittman cracked a smile.

"Pitt, I think you're my best friend," Rabbit said, wiping a tear out of his eye with his free hand.

"God help me," Pitt chuckled.

Socks and I went to the filing cabinet. "Not locked," Socks said, then looked at the Warden. "Some top-notch security you got here, dickhead." That set Rabbit off again.

We started to look through the files. I found Byrdie's, but I skipped over it. No point in picking at an open wound.

"I found Noel," Socks said, pulling out a file. He started to flip through pages, and I waited. "Wow, whoever wrote this is an idiot. There's like ten typos. What kind of Department is this? She was arrested for murdering her boyfriend, says something about domestic abuse—"

"You assholes arrested a girl for killing her abusive boyfriend?" Pittman snapped. He moved his gun so that it was level with the Warden's head.

"I'm—I'm not a cop," the Warden said, for the first time, sounding nervous. He still didn't look it.

"She had a daughter," Socks said, looking up at us. "She's three, her name is Jewel." I felt like someone had punched me in the stomach.

"Fuck me, man," Rabbit said, shaking his head. "Look for someone else, I don't wanna hear about this."

I didn't want to think about a little girl, motherless. But I couldn't help it. I saw a sweet little black girl, her hair wrapped up like Noel's was, strutting into Pre-K. I saw her laughing, her rolling her eyes like her mom did. I wondered who was taking care of her. Maybe a grandmother.

"Heather?"

It was Socks. "Yeah," I said, shaking my head a little. "I'm good." The first file I saw was Rabbits. I pulled it out. "I got you, Jack," I smiled before flipping it open.

"Arrested for selling drugs," I read. "Wow, you really don't like being confined, do you? Two attempted escapes and one successful one. Good for you."

"Not bad," Socks said. "Does he have a middle name?"

Rabbit shifted the gun so it was pointed at me. "Don't you dare," he said. I closed the file and set it on top of the cabinet.

"So touchy," I joked. I realized I was probably being too casual, but we were having fun. The four of us were genuinely enjoying ourselves. That should have scared me more than it did.

"Please, if you just—" the Warden said. Rabbit put his gun back on him. I had almost forgotten he was still in the room.

"Shut the fuck up, dickhead, we're in the middle of something," Rabbit said. "Find someone else."

Socks and I went back to looking. There must have been a thousand files in there. Finally, Socks tapped my hand. I looked up at him. He was holding my file.

"Aw, fuck," Rabbit said, hopping from one foot to the other. "I've been waiting like a year for this."

"Like, six months, tops," Pittman corrected.

I looked at the file for a second. I was finally going to know why I ended up here. I opened it to the first page. It had all of my information, like the other files had. My name, age, height, birthday—all generic stuff. Under charges, there was just three marks.

N/A.

I shook my head. I looked at the original date of arrest. Another N/A.

Not applicable.

I looked up at the Warden. "What the fuck does this mean?" I asked. He didn't look at me. I threw the file at him. "What does this *mean*?" I yelled.

"What?" Socks asked.

"It just says N/A on it," I said, "I didn't do anything."

I felt like everyone held their breath. "What does it mean?" I shouted louder this time. Rabbit took a few steps forward, leaned over the desk, and touched the gun to the Warden's forehead.

"She asked you a question, dickhead."

The Warden was visibly shaking. I didn't care. I wasn't going to ask him again. He swallowed hard, and then without moving his head, looked at me. "The Department of Prisoner Welfare and Psychology—we—they—it was decided that— to truly test the, um, the system that we—they, ugh—"

"Spit it out, dickhead," Rabbit said, pressing the gun so hard against his forehead that the Warden was pushed back against his seat.

"They decided that in order to test the progression of the population, they should mix in a few non-criminals, to see how everyone adjusted," the Warden said, all too quickly.

"The fuck?" Pittman said for everyone.

"*We*? You're a part of this department?" I asked him. I snatched my file back from his lap. "When we first got here, you said that the people who put us in 917 were jailed. Was that bullshit?"

The Warden didn't say anything.

"Dude, if I shoot you from here, I'm going to get brains all over me," Rabbit said. "Just answer her."

The Warden shook his head no.

"So they were jailed?"

"They were fired."

"*Just* fired?" I snapped. "We were living in our own shit and they got *fired*?"

"I wonder what that pension looks like," Socks said, shaking his head.

"So what was the plan with us?" I yelled. "What is wrong with you people?"

"We—they were going to try to reintroduce some of you, see if you could be civilized again, but then they had to send in a rescue team, so everyone had to be reintroduced at once, it wasn't supposed to be this way, we—"

"We? *We?*" I snapped. "Rabbit."

Rabbit pulled the gun away from his head and shot him in the knee.

A loud pop, and the Warden screamed. "We were trying to help you!" he yelled, clutching his leg. A red circle of blood was spreading through his pants leg. "We didn't put you there, we were trying to save you!"

"And what, bring us here?" Rabbit yelled. "Motherfucker, you can't fuck up this badly and not know it."

I looked at Socks. Rabbit and Pitt were a bit off the rails at the moment. I was too. I needed someone else. "Even if he was trying to help, it doesn't make up for it," Socks said.

"So," I said, taking a deep breath in. "You didn't put us there. Alright. It was the other people, the old people. That prison is old. I get it. But you knew we were there. Suffering. What did you do to help us?"

The Warden looked up at me. "I took you in."

"You took us in because we—because *I* forced your hand. What did you do to help us?" I looked at him, really looked at him. I don't know how to describe the look in his eyes. It wasn't begging, or pain. It was almost acceptance. Like he knew what he did was wrong, and he knew he was fucked now.

"I tried to get them to move the reintroduction up, to—"

"That would only help some of us. What did you do to help *all* of us," I repeated.

The Warden writhed in pain. "Nothing."

"What about Heather?" Pittman asked. "What did you do about innocents being thrown in with us?"

"Nothing," he sobbed.

I paused. "Wait, who else is innocent?" I couldn't have been the only one.

The Warden took in a breath. "A little girl, she came in with you, I—"

"Byrdie?" Rabbit cut him off. "No, she killed her sister. She told everyone about it."

The Warden was clutching his leg so tightly his entire arms were turning white. "No, they convinced her she did. If you speak to anyone long enough, you can convince them of

85

crimes they didn't commit. We wanted to see how it would affect her growing up."

My entire body was shaking. I wasn't angry. I felt an intense pain in my chest, like someone was sitting on it. "Byrdie died because of that," I said, quietly. "She was burned alive because you told a six-year-old she murdered her baby sister."

Socks reached out to touch me, and I pulled my arm away from him so violently, I smashed it into the filing cabinet. "Who else?" I asked him.

The Warden took in a deep breath. "Ugh, a few people over the years."

"Tell me."

"I don't remember!"

Rabbit moved to put the gun on his other knee. "You'd best."

"Ugh, um," the Warden stammered. "Mickey-Something, a transgirl, Tyrone Jenkins, um."

"Tyrone?" Pittman repeated. We all looked at him. "He was a Pink. Someone stabbed him at a Green's garden. Died three days later."

"Who else?" I pushed.

"Um, George something, Cynthia Garcia, ugh, um—"

"Not your George, right?" Socks asked Pitt.

He shook his head. "No, George was picked up for solicitation, then fought a chomo and got transferred to us," he said, confident. Socks wasn't. He turned and started looking for his file.

"So Delany wasn't the only innocent one," Rabbit said in awe. "I knew there was something off about you, Red."

"Anyone else?" I asked the Warden.

"Maybe before my time, I don't remember."

"Found it," Socks announced, turning around with the file in his hand. He flipped it open and took a few seconds to read it. "So, good news. He *did* fight a child molester, and he *was* a prostitute," Socks said. "But doesn't look like he was charged—yeah, they picked him up out of a rehab center for abused kids. He wasn't picked up for any crime though. Original arrest date is N/A."

I looked over at Pittman. He was usually a hard person to read and now was no exception. He barely blinked. "We can kill him after this, if you want," Rabbit offered. "Got plenty of bullets."

"No, no," Pittman said softly. "It's alright."

"He probably just figured he did," I said. "He might have thought he just forgot because of the drugs, or repressed it, or was high or something. It doesn't mean he lied on purpose."

"Or he just said it to fit in," Socks added. "Very few people have maintained their innocence the whole time. Don't worry about it."

Pittman nodded. "It's fine. I'm good."

"Please," the Warden said, drawing our attention back to him. I was shocked he hadn't put up any hint of a fight.

Rabbit was close enough to him he probably could have tried to wrestle the gun away from him at some point. "I need medical attention."

I realized everyone was looking at me, waiting. I didn't know what to say. After months of all of this—four months in 917, a month at the other prison, and two months at 456—I didn't know what to say. I saw two people fight until they were bloodied and broken over stale bread. I saw Delany scratch herself bloody trying to get out of a cell. I saw dead bodies, and too many ribs to count. I saw a dead baby, just a few days old. I saw an innocent six-year-old girl burned to death. I was tired and sweaty and dirty—maybe our suffering wasn't his fault, but he didn't do anything to stop it.

"Rabbit, shoot him."

Rabbit leaned back, held the gun up to the Warden's head, and shot him dead.